Izzy and Poe
by Anita Felicelli

Henflower Press
2013

Library of Congress Control Number: 2013921263
ISBN-13: 978-0-9857313-4-2

Izzy and Poe

by Anita Felicelli
Pictures by Lindsay Merrill

Henflower Press
2013

for dreamers
especially the real Izzy
and Poe
and Illyria

One afternoon, Izzy and Poe rolled around in the autumn leaves. They chased rabbits out of the vegetable patch. They were bored with chewing bones.

Time for an adventure!

"Are you done reading yet?" Izzy asked the girl.

"Can we go to the beach?" asked Poe.

"Yes," said the girl. "But promise me, no barking at the hang gliders. And play nice with the other dogs."

"We promise," they said.

They ran down the trail to the beach. Dogs jumped through the salty air. They bounded into the ocean with Frisbees in their mouths. Hang gliders flew above them like seagulls.

Four horses walked by and Izzy barked at them.

Woof! Woof!

Poe stayed at the edge of the water with the girl. "I don't want a bath," he said.

A big wave chased him. The girl unwrapped kelp from his paws.

Poe and the girl followed Izzy as she kicked up sand and splashed in the waves.

Woof! Woof!

Poe barked at hang gliders. "I want to fly, too!" he said.

"Where is our adventure?"
Izzy asked the girl.

Just then, someone yelled,
"Captain Jack! Come back
here!"

They looked up and saw a
green parrot flapping its wings.
A guy was sprinting towards the
parrot. He shook his fist.

Whoosh! The parrot flew up a grassy hill.

"Poe, look! Our adventure!" said Izzy. She chased the parrot.

"Wait for me," said Poe, "I want to have an adventure, too."

"STOP!" shouted the girl.

"STOP!" shouted the guy.

They ran along the edge of a cliff. The beach was far below. The dogs and horses looked as tiny as ants.

"Izzy, I'm tired," said Poe. He looked around. The girl and the guy were nowhere to be seen.

"Where's Captain Jack?" asked Izzy.

"Up here, you dogs, so slow and so small! I'm up in a tree. Can't catch me," squawked the parrot.

"Where are you going?" asked Poe.

"Can we come?" asked Izzy.

"Only if you learn how to fly. Want to try?" said Captain Jack.

He flew around them. "No tails? No wings? Funny-looking things!"

"We don't look funny," said Izzy.

"I want wings," said Poe.

"Me, too. How do we get them?" asked Izzy.

"Hang gliders wear wings. They rule the air like kings," said Captain Jack. "Do we dare make you a pair?"

The parrot hopped around, hunting for branches.

"We didn't promise not to fly," said Izzy.

"We didn't promise not to wear wings," said Poe.

"Think of the places we could fly," said Izzy. She jumped around. "We could go anywhere. London! Cairo! The North Pole!"

"I've always wanted to go to Iowa," said Poe.

"Well, don't just stand there. Find branches with leaves so you can fly through the air," said Captain Jack.

The parrot found four branches with lots of leaves. He tied the branches to their collars. "You see? Now you're ready for a flying lesson from me," he said.

"I like these wings," said Izzy.

Poe was worried. "Do you think they will really help us fly?"

"Of course, oh wow! You're all ready now," said Captain Jack. "Follow me, if you want to be free!"

"Maybe we should wait for our girl," Izzy said, looking around.

"Don't be a scaredy-cat! A split and a splat and you'll be over the waves!" said the parrot. "Just use the wings I've made!"

Izzy and Poe followed him to the edge of the cliff. A gust of wind caught their wings. It lifted them into the air.

"We're flying," shouted Izzy. Magic!

But then Izzy looked down. Her feet sank back into the grass.

A hang glider soared by. He shouted, "Where's your girl?" Izzy and Poe could barely hear him over the sound of the wind. "Stay away from the edge! It's dangerous."

"Don't listen to that party-pooper. That no-good snooper." said the parrot.

Izzy and Poe looked at each other. They were dizzy from looking at the waves.

"Um, your wings don't look like the hang glider's wings, Poe," said Izzy.

"I don't think these wings can hold us up," said Poe.

But the parrot said, "Yes they can. At least that's the plan. Flap just like me. Away we'll go — Whee!"

"Izzy! Poe!"

Izzy and Poe looked back. The girl and guy ran towards them.

"Bad bird!" the guy said.

"Bad bird, Bad bird. That's all I've heard," said the parrot.

"You're up to your usual naughty tricks, I see," said the guy.

"I should have known my fun would be blown," said the parrot.

The girl hugged Izzy and Poe. She said, "I was so worried! And what are those things on your heads?"

"Wings!" said Izzy.

"We wanted to fly," said Poe.

"You're dogs," said the girl. "Dogs run. But please don't ever run so far away again."

"Captain Jack says we look funny," said Izzy.

The girl turned to the bird. "Well, where are your front legs? Can't run as fast as dogs can, can you?"

The parrot pecked the guy's head. For once he had nothing to say.

The guy said, "Sorry about my bird. I hope I see you again soon."

"Me too," said the girl.

The guy and his parrot turned and disappeared into the grass.

Izzy, Poe and their girl jogged back along the trail. It was dark by the time they got home. The girl gave Izzy and Poe warm milk and a plate of peanut butter-bacon cookies.

"Do we look funny?" asked Izzy as she drank the milk.

"You're beautiful dogs," said the girl.

"Are we scaredy-cats?" asked Poe munching on a cookie.

"No, you're just right," said the girl.

"For a second, we flew," said Poe.

"It was magic," said Izzy.

"Magic is the best," said the girl and turned out the light.

In the dark, Izzy whispered, "Poe?"

"What?" said Poe. He was sleepy.

"Next time let's try an even bigger adventure," said Izzy.

"Like what?"

Izzy said, "Oh, there are millions of things we could do. Let's swim to the North Pole."

THE END

Anita Felicelli is a novelist, essayist and poet who lives in the San Francisco Bay Area with her husband, daughter, and the real-life Izzy and Poe. Her writing has appeared in the New York Times, Brain Child, Babble, Los Angeles Review of Books and elsewhere. Her first novel SPARKS OFF YOU was a 2012 ForeWord Books of the Year (YA) finalist.

Lindsay Merrill is a California native. She received her degree in Fine Arts from Carnegie Mellon University in 2009. She has illustrated several books including Manuel Marticorena Quintanilla's poetry collection EVOCACIONES (Evocations), as well as TRAVESURAS AMAZÓNICAS (Amazonian Mischief), a collection of children's stories written by Ana Ríos Gonzales. She currently lives in Pittsburgh, PA.

CPSIA information can be obtained
at www.ICGtesting.com
Printed in the USA
LVIC01n1940041213
363915LV00004B/4